WINDOWS OF GOLD
and other Golden Tales

WINDOWS
OF GOLD
and other Golden Tales

RETOLD BY SELMA G. LANES

ILLUSTRATED BY KIMBERLY BULCKEN ROOT

Simon and Schuster Books for Young Readers

Published by Simon & Schuster Inc., New York

To The Singing Lady and memories
of a Thirties' childhood.
S. G. L.

To my grandparents
K.B.R.

SIMON AND SCHUSTER BOOKS FOR YOUNG READERS, Simon & Schuster Building, Rockefeller Center, 1230
Avenue of the Americas, New York, New York 10020.   Text copyright © 1989 retold by Selma G. Lanes. Illustrations
copyright © 1989 by Kimberly Bulcken Root. All rights reserved including the right of reproduction in whole or in part in
any form.   SIMON AND SCHUSTER BOOKS FOR YOUNG READERS is a trademark of Simon & Schuster Inc.
Manufactured in the United States of America

10 9 8 7 6 5 4 3 2 1

Library of Congress Cataloging-in-Publication Data: Lanes, Selma G.   Windows of gold and other golden tales.
Summary: The magical properties of gold spark an anthology of stories from around the world, in which gold can make
dreams come true or turn fortune into folly.   1. Children's stories, American.   [1. Gold—Fiction.   2. Short stories.]
I. Root, Kimberly Bulcken, ill.   II. Title.   PZ7.L25125Wi   1989   88-4464

ISBN 0-671-64377-0

TABLE OF CONTENTS

WINDOWS OF GOLD
(American)

nce upon a time at the bottom of a high hill, there lived a widow and her small son Harry. They were poor as church mice, but the mother did fine sewing and, in this way, earned money enough to keep a cottage roof over their heads and simple food on their table.

Whenever the sun shone, Harry played outside the cottage, while his mother worked at her sewing indoors. Though he had no toys, still Harry managed with sticks and stones to amuse himself quite well. Best of all, Harry liked to gaze up to the top of the high hill.

There he saw a cottage much like his own. It had just one difference: the cottage at the top of the hill had windows all made of gold! How they gleamed in the mid-morning sunlight, and how Harry wished that he and his mother might live in such a grand place themselves.

One bright and cloudless day, when Harry and his mother were just finishing their lunch of bread and milk, the boy had an idea. Instead of playing outside the cottage as usual this afternoon he would go exploring. Harry decided to make a long trip up the high hill. He would visit the house with the windows all made of gold.

His mind made up, Harry stepped into the dirt road not far from the cottage door. If he turned to the right, the boy knew that the road led into town. He had made this trip with his mother many times. But, if he turned to the left, the road wound round and round the high hill until, at last, it reached the very top. Harry had never made that trip. None the less, he was determined to do so now.

Harry walked, and walked, and walked until at last he came within sight of the cottage at the top of the hill. Outside of it, Harry could see a girl his own size playing with a rag doll. When the child caught sight of Harry, she ran towards him. Visitors were few so far from town, and the girl, whose name was Sally, was overjoyed to see a boy her own age.

"She must be a princess," thought Harry to himself, "to live in such a house with windows all made of gold." But where were the golden windows he had come so far to see? Now that he was here, Harry saw only that the cottage looked even more like his own: Its windows were not made of gold, but of glass — exactly like his own!

"Who are you?" asked Sally. "From where do you come?"

"I'm Harry," he told her. "And I come from the cottage at the bottom of the hill."

The little girl's eyes opened wide as she pointed down towards Harry's cottage. "From the house with the windows all made of gold?" she asked.

Harry thought she might be making fun of him, but he turned toward his own house, far off in the distance. There, at the bottom of the hill it was, much like the one where he now stood. It had just one difference: Harry's cottage had windows all made of gold!

How could that be? What magic took place while Harry was walking from the bottom of the hill to the top?

Sun magic. Every morning when Harry looked up the high hill, he saw the sun's golden rays reflected in the windows of the cottage at the top. And every afternoon when Sally looked down the high hill, she saw the sun's golden rays reflected in the windows of the cottage at the bottom.

If Sally was a princess, then Harry was a prince! The sun had crowned them both. But Harry and Sally became something else that day —friends. Now, they took turns visiting one another. And, whether they were at the bottom of the hill or at the top, they could always look off into the distance and see a house with windows all made of gold!

NINE WISE MEN OF GOTHAM
(English)

Once upon a time, the village of Gotham in England was known far and wide for the wisdom of its inhabitants. And one bright morning, nine such wise men of Gotham went fishing in the sea.

Three of them stood well back on the shore and, casting their lines far into the water, did their fishing that way. Three others stood at the water's edge and, with shorter lines, did their fishing this way. The last three wise men walked hip-deep into the sea and did their fishing in that fashion.

By the end of the day, each man had caught a good number of fish and turned happily toward home.

"What an adventure this has been!" said one man.

"And what luck that none of us is drowned," said another.

"Too true," replied a third.

"Yet how can we be sure?" asked a fourth.

"Perhaps we'd better stop right here and count ourselves," suggested a fifth wise man.

So stop they did, and each man carefully counted all his companions. But not one wise man of Gotham remembered to count himself!

"Lord, have mercy!" they cried. "Only eight of us are here. One of us is drowned."

As one man, the wise men of Gotham turned and ran back to the sea. They searched up and down the shore, but they found nobody.

"Woe be unto us!" they moaned. "One of us is surely drowned."

And every wise man of Gotham sat down upon the sand and wept.

Soon a traveler on horseback came upon the sobbing group. "Good sirs!" he called out in alarm. "What is the cause of this pitiable caterwauling?"

"Alack! Alas! and woe is us!" they answered. "This day nine of us came down to the sea to fish, and now one of us is drowned."

"Bless me!" said the horseman. "Are you sure?"

Again, each wise man rose and counted every other man of Gotham but himself. This the traveler saw at once.

"Such a pity!" said the horseman, pretending to wipe away a tear. "What, say you, would be the reward, were some miracle to restore your unfortunate companion?"

"All the gold that is in our purses!" cried one wise man of Gotham. "And all the fish that we have caught as well," offered another.

The traveler told them to put all their money in one pile, and their fresh fish in another. Then, starting with the fisherman closest to him, the horseman began to count.

"One!" he said and gave the first man of Gotham a stout whack with his riding whip. That wise man cried out in pain. "So much for Number One," the traveler said.

This same thing he repeated with each and every man of Gotham as he counted.

When he came to the last fisherman, the horseman shouted "NINE!" and struck so sound a blow that the ninth wise man fell to the sand.

"Aha!" said the horseman. "Here, large as life, is your ninth man, alive and well after all."

"Marvelous!" exclaimed one wise man of Gotham.

"Incredible!" said another.

"Miraculous!" proclaimed the rest.

And, as the ninth man of Gotham rose from the sand in wonderment, they all stood about congratulating each other on their unbelievable good fortune.

The man on horseback, meanwhile, picked up his gold and his fish, and rode off well pleased with his own bit of luck.

Surely so strange and happy an adventure could have befallen none but nine such wise men of Gotham!

PUSS IN BOOTS
(French)

Once upon a time, there lived a poor miller who had three sons. To the eldest, he left his mill, to the second son his donkey and to the youngest nothing but the Cat. Poor lad!

Luckily, it was no ordinary Cat.

"Do not worry, Master," said the Cat. "Only get me a strong sack, and a pair of boots made just for me so that I can run where I will without getting scratched, and I can make your fortune."

When the Cat got what he asked for, he pulled on his new boots and threw the sack over his shoulder. Straightaway he went to a place where he had seen a great number of young rabbits. He sprinkled bran and tender clover into his sack, which he now opened wide, and stretched himself out on the ground as if he were dead.

Soon several silly young rabbits jumped into the sack to feast, and Mr. Puss pulled the drawstrings closed. Proud of his catch, Puss went directly to the Palace and asked to speak with the King.

Taken before His Majesty, he said: "Sire, I bring you six tender little rabbits from my master, the Marquis of Carabas." (Slyboots had made up that name on the spot.) "He commanded me to make Your Honor a present of them."

"Tell your master that I am well pleased," said the King. Rabbit happened to be his favorite dish.

Soon after, Puss went and hid among the cornstalks with his open sack. This time he scattered corn meal inside. When a heedless brace of partridges ran into the bag to nibble, once more Puss pulled the drawstrings tight and carried the unfortunate creatures to the King.

Again, His Majesty was well pleased. He began to think kindly toward this unknown Marquis of Carabas.

The Cat continued in like manner over the next several weeks, carrying tasty tidbits to the king in the name of his Master, the Marquis of Carabas. Then, on a day when he learned that the King and his beautiful daughter were to drive by the riverside, Puss ordered his Master to go and wash himself in the river.

"Do this, and leave the rest to me," said the Cat. "Your fortune is as good as made!"

Without knowing why or wherefore, the poor miller's youngest son did as Puss asked. While he was washing in the river, the King drove by, and the Cat began to cry out as loud as he could: "Help! Help! My Lord, the Marquis of Carabas, is going to drown."

When the King recognized the Puss who had brought him such delicacies, he ordered his guard to run and help the unfortunate Marquis of Carabas.

Meanwhile, the Cat came up to the King's coach and told a sad tale: While his master was washing, several robbers had run off with his clothes. (That rogue of a Cat had simply hidden his master's poor rags under a stone.) The King at once ordered his footman to run and fetch one of his best suits for the unfortunate Marquis of Carabas.

When, at last, the miller's son walked up to the coach dressed in the King's finery, he was as handsome a pauper as ever lived. The Princess fell immediately in love with him, and the King invited the elegant Marquis of Carabas to ride with them.

The Cat, enchanted to see his plan working so well, ran ahead and, meeting with some countrymen mowing a meadow, he said to them: "Good mowers, if you do not tell the King that the meadow you mow belongs to my Lord, the Marquis of Carabas, then you shall be chopped as fine as sliced onions for his stew!"

When the King passed and asked whose meadow they mowed, the frightened peasants answered, "Our Lord, the Marquis of Carabas." The poor miller's son nodded modestly, and the Princess smiled adoringly.

Meanwhile, the Cat had run farther ahead where he met with some reapers. To them he said: "Good reapers, if you do not tell the King that the fields you reap belong to my Lord, the Marquis of Carabas, then you will be chopped as fine as mincemeat for his pie!"

When the King passed a few minutes later and asked whose fields were being reaped, the peasants answered, "Those of our Lord, the Marquis of Carabas." The King was pleased by this reply.

As always the Cat kept well ahead of the King's carriage, so that the King was soon astonished to learn how vast was the property of his passenger, the Marquis of Carabas.

At last the Cat came to a large castle, which he knew belonged to the richest Ogre who ever lived. (In truth, all the lands that the King had ridden past belonged to this same giant.) Puss knocked boldly at the Ogre's door. He wished, he said, to pay his respects.

The Ogre received Puss as nicely as an Ogre could. "I have been told," said the Cat, "that you can change yourself into any large creature – for example, an elephant, or the like."

"True," said the Ogre. And to convince the Cat, he turned himself into a lion forthwith.

"Remarkable!" said the Cat when the Ogre took his natural form again. "But I don't suppose, good Sire, that you can as well take on the shape of some small creature – say a rat, or even a mouse. Impossible, I'd think."

"Impossible?" shouted the Ogre. "You shall see."

With that, he changed himself into a field mouse that scampered across the floor. The Cat no sooner saw this than he pounced and ate the mouse on the spot.

Meanwhile the King had reached the castle and decided to pay a call. Hearing the wheels of the royal coach in the courtyard, the Cat ran out and said: "Welcome, Your Majesty, to this humble home of my Lord, the Marquis of Carabas."

"What, my Lord Marquis," said the King, "does this grand castle also belong to you? Let us enter, if you please."

The miller's son gave his arm to the Princess. In the great hall, they found a magnificent meal, which the Ogre had prepared for his own afternoon snack. The King was charmed by the thoughtfulness — and the wealth — of the Marquis of Carabas. As was his daughter.

After they had eaten their fill, the King said that he would have no objection to so handsome and rich a son-in-law as the Marquis of Carabas. On his part, the miller's son made several low bows and accepted the honor. He and the Princess were married that day. As for the Cat, he became a great Lord and never ran after mice again — except for his own amusement.

THE MILKMAID AND HER JUG
(Greek)

nce upon a time, a milkmaid walked to market carrying her milk in a big jug on top of her head. As she went along, she began to think about how she would spend the money she got for her milk.

"First," said she, "I'll buy some eggs from Farmer Brown. Then, I'll put them under the little red hen who will hatch me a lot of little chicks of my own.

"And my little chicks will all grow up to be hens who will lay dozens of eggs for me!

"Next, I'll sell all my eggs for a lot of money," she said. "Then, with the money I get from my eggs, I'll buy me a beautiful white dress and a hat with pink flowers and blue ribbons.

"How grand I'll look when I go to market in my new white dress and hat with pink flowers and blue ribbons!

"And won't just about everybody gather round to look at me? Sally Shaw will stand there and stare. Molly Malone will stop and gawk. Even Jack Squires will tip his cap to me.

"As for me, I shall just walk past them all. I shall hold my chin high and toss back my head."

And as she spoke, the milkmaid tossed her head back proudly. The jug fell off her head and broke, and all the milk inside it was spilled. The poor milkmaid had nothing to sell, and all her fine dreams came to nothing as well. Worse, she had to go home and tell her mother what had happened.

"Daughter, daughter," said the milkmaid's mother. "Never count your chickens before they are hatched!"

KING MIDAS AND THE GOLDEN TOUCH
(Greek)

nce upon a time, there lived a king named Midas who loved gold. He loved gold more than anything else – except perhaps his only child, the Princess Marigold. Even so, he spent more time in the counting house under his royal palace than he did in the company of his beloved daughter Marigold.

Every day, right after breakfast, King Midas took the key to his counting house out of his royal trousers' pocket and walked briskly down the back stairs of the palace. After opening the great counting house door, Midas went quickly inside and locked it behind him.

One by one, the King emptied out his sacks of gold. When Midas finished counting each and every gold coin in one sack, he took another. To empty all the sacks into one great pile took a week. To put all the gold coins back into each and every sack took another week.

King Midas loved the look of gold. King Midas loved the feel of gold. And King Midas loved the sound of gold, one coin clinking against another, as he counted and recounted his treasure.

One morning, while the King sat among his sacks of gold pieces, a shadow fell across his heap of coins. When Midas looked up, he saw before him a handsome young stranger, aglow in a golden light.

Now King Midas had the only key to the counting house, so he knew that this was no ordinary mortal. At once, the greedy King wondered what special favor this magical being might be able to grant.

"How rich you are, King Midas!" the stranger said.

"True, I have lots of gold," King Midas answered sadly. "But not nearly as much as I should like."

"You are not satisfied?" the young man asked.

Midas shook his head.

"What then, would make you content?" the stranger asked.

Midas thought carefully. Should he ask for a golden mountain? Or a great river of liquid gold? But how troublesome it would be to count such treasures. At last, Midas had an idea.

"I wish," he said, "that everything I touch could turn into gold."

"Ah, the Golden Touch," the stranger said, smiling. "Are you sure that this would make you happy?"

"Nothing else," said King Midas, "could make me half so content."

"Done then!" said the young man with a wave of the hand. "Tomorrow, when you wake up, the Golden Touch will be yours!"

The stranger's figure grew so bright that Midas closed his eyes. When he opened them again, the visitor had vanished. Midas wasn't sure he hadn't been dreaming.

That afternoon, King Midas and Princess Marigold took their daily walk in the palace garden, which was famous for its roses. Marigold loved these flowers as much as her father loved gold. Later, father and daughter ate their royal supper and went to bed.

When Midas awoke next morning, he threw back his blanket and found, to his delight, that it changed to gold as soon as his fingers touched it. The King rose and tapped the royal bedpost. It too turned to gold. As Midas dressed, each piece of clothing was transformed into finest golden cloth. He picked up a favorite handkerchief that Marigold had sewn for him. It, too, became gold!

King Midas reached for his spectacles, the better to see his new riches. But, once they were on, he saw nothing. His glasses had turned to gold! This last change annoyed Midas. Still, what a wondrous gift he possessed!

As King Midas walked downstairs, the bannisters turned immediately to gold, as did each step as soon as his foot touched it.

Midas walked out into his rose garden. How glorious was the fragrance of roses in the morning air. The King could not resist walking from bush to bush, transforming every flower and bud — even a bumble bee resting on a rose petal — into purest gold.

Well pleased with his work, Midas now went inside to eat. A footman quickly brought in his royal bowl of oatmeal, some freshly boiled eggs, toast and a cup of steaming-hot coffee.

Just then, the King heard Princess Marigold approaching. She was sobbing bitterly — which was unusual. The princess hardly shed a thimble-ful of tears from January to December.

When Midas heard her sobs, he decided to give the Princess a nice surprise. He touched her china oatmeal bowl — a pretty one with painted figures all around it — and, at once, it was gleaming gold.

Marigold came in, holding one of Midas's golden roses.

"How beautiful!" said the King.

"It is the ugliest flower that ever grew!" said Marigold, stamping her royal foot. "What's more, every other rose is spoiled as well. What ever is the matter?"

"Now, now!" said the King, a bit hurt. "You can exchange any one of these golden roses for a garden full of the old kind. Do sit down and eat your porridge."

"I hate these roses!" cried Marigold, throwing hers to the floor. "They have no smell, and their hard petals scratch my nose!" The Princess was so upset that she didn't even notice her golden bowl.

Midas, meanwhile, raised his coffee cup to his lips. It turned at once to gold. But how astonished the King was to find that no sooner had the dark liquid touched his lips than it, too, turned to molten gold.

"Ouch!" Midas cried, for it burned his mouth.

"What's wrong, father?" asked Marigold.

"Nothing, child, nothing at all," said Midas crossly. "Eat your oatmeal before it gets cold."

Now Midas tried an egg. It turned to gold before he had even cracked the shell. By this time, the King was quite famished.

Next, Midas tried popping a bit of toast directly into his open mouth and then swallowing it quickly. No luck! He almost choked on a solid lump of gold. The King jumped up in fright.

"Father, dear Father!" cried Marigold running to his side.

Suddenly, Midas knew that Marigold's love was worth a thousand Golden Touches.

"My precious," murmured the King as he took her hand.

Marigold said no more. No sooner had Midas touched her than Marigold turned to gold. A golden tear glistened on one golden cheek. His beloved living, breathing child was nothing but a golden statue!

How the foolish King wept! When he felt sure his heart would burst, Midas lifted his head and saw, once again, the stranger standing before him.

"Fortunate Midas!" he said, smiling. "How fares the King with the Golden Touch?"

"Miserably," replied the King.

"Have I not kept my promise?" asked the stranger. "And have you not exactly what your heart desired?"

"Because of my foolish Golden Touch," the King said sadly, "I have lost what was dearest to my heart. Gold is not everything."

"Ah," said the stranger, at once interested. "Which, in your opinion, is worth more — the Golden Touch or a cup of clear, cold water?"

"Oh, blessed water!" cried the thirsty Midas.

"The Golden Touch or a crust of bread?" persisted the young man.

"A piece of bread," said the hungry Midas, "is worth all the gold in my counting house."

"The Golden Touch," continued the stranger, "or your own little Marigold as she was just a short hour ago?"

"Oh, my child, my poor child!" sobbed Midas. "I would not trade the dimple on her chin for all the gold in the world."

"Think carefully," said the stranger. "Do you sincerely wish to be rid of the Golden Touch?"

"It is hateful to me!" Midas cried.

"Go then," said the stranger. "Plunge into the river at the foot of your garden. Then take a pitcher full of its water, and sprinkle it over each and every object you may wish to change back to its original state."

The King bowed in gratitude and, when he lifted his head, the shining stranger was gone.

Midas hurried to the river, golden pitcher in hand. He dove into the water and, as soon as he came up for air, carefully filled the container with water.

The pitcher changed back into pottery before the delighted King's eyes. Hurrying back to the palace, Midas first sprinkled a handful of water over Marigold.

No sooner did the water touch her than Marigold once more became a living, breathing child. Arms outstretched, she hugged her father. She remembered nothing of being turned into gold.

Together, Midas and Marigold sprinkled water over each and every rosebush. How delighted they both were to see and smell the real flowers! With the remaining drops, Midas returned all else to its former state.

King Midas never forgot the terrible day of the Golden Touch. When he grew quite old, he told the story to Princess Marigold's children, just as you are hearing it now. Sometimes the King would stroke the golden curls on their heads as he spoke.

"To tell the truth," he said, "ever since that dreadful day, I shudder at the sight of any gold but that on your own dear heads."

THE SMALL RABBIT WHO WANTED EVERYTHING
(Afro-American)

Once upon a time, there was a Small Rabbit with one fluffy white cottontail, two long, pinkish ears, two bright red eyes and four soft furry paws. She was as pretty a Small Rabbit as you could hope to see. But she wasn't satisfied.

When Mr. Bushy Tail, the grey squirrel, ran by, Small Rabbit would cry, "Oh, Mother dear, how I wish I had a long grey tail like Mr. Bushy Tail's instead of this small white puff I call my own."

And when Mr. Prickles, the porcupine, walked by, Small Rabbit would sigh and say, "Oh, Mother dear, now I wish I had a back full of bristles like Mr. Prickles', instead of this plain brown coat I call my own."

And when Mistress Quack, the duck, waddled by in her two little red rubbers, Small Rabbit would whine and wail, "Oh, Mother dear, how I wish I had a pair of red rubbers like Mistress Quack's, instead of these soft furry paws I call my own."

In this way, she went on wishing and wanting, and she might be wanting and wishing still if Old Mr. Groundhog hadn't overheard her one day.

Now Old Mr. Groundhog was smart, and he said to Small Rabbit: "Go on down to the Wishing Pool, look at yourself in the water, then turn around three times and you'll get yourself whatever it is you wish."

Now Small Rabbit did not have to be told twice. Off she hopped until she came to the Wishing Pool in the hollow stump of an old sycamore tree. A little yellow bird was perched at the pool's edge getting a drink.

As soon as Small Rabbit saw the yellow bird, she began wishing again. "Oh, how I wish I had a pair of little yellow wings," she said to herself. At the same instant, she looked into the Wishing Pool and saw her own face. Then, remembering what Old Mr. Groundhog had told her, she turned around three times.

Suddenly, she had a most peculiar feeling in her shoulders. Sure enough, she looked and saw yellow wings bursting through! She sat all day in the woods by the Wishing Pool, waiting for the yellow wings to finish growing.

By and by, when it was almost sundown, she ran home to show her mother the beautiful yellow wings. But guess what? Her mother didn't recognize her! In all her born days, she had never seen a rabbit with yellow wings, and she wasn't about to let one into her rabbit hole.

Neither would Mr. Bushy Tail, Mr. Prickles or Mistress Quack let Small Rabbit sleep at their houses. Not until she came with her yellow wings to Old Mr. Groundhog's house did Small Rabbit find a welcome. He was smart enough to figure out exactly what had happened. But Old Mr. Groundhog had beech nuts spread all over the floor of his house, and Small Rabbit slept poorly.

When morning came, she decided to try out her new yellow wings. She hopped to the top of a hill, spread the new flappers and sailed off.

Soon she landed kerplunk in a bush full of thorns. Her four furry paws kept getting caught so that she couldn't pull herself out.

"Mother! Mother!" cried Small Rabbit. "Help me! HELP!"

Her mother couldn't hear her, but Old Mr. Groundhog did. He came to help Small Rabbit get free. "Not bad for a first flight," he said. "You'll get used to those yellow wings in no time."

"Don't want them," mumbled Small Rabbit.

"Well then," said Old Mr. Groundhog, "I suppose you might try wishing them off at the Wishing Pool just the same way you wished them on."

Small Rabbit didn't have to be told twice. Back she hopped to the Wishing Pool in double quick time. No sooner did she see her face than she turned around three times and, sure enough, those yellow wings were gone!

Now she ran home to her mother as fast as four furry paws could carry her. This time her mother recognized her right away. She was delighted to have her home. Never again did Small Rabbit hop about wanting or wishing for anything that belonged to somebody else. She was glad enough to be her own self.

THE GOLDEN BIRD
(German)

nce upon a time, there was a king who had in his palace garden a remarkable tree. It grew golden apples. One day when the apples were almost ripe, the King counted them. Next morning when he looked again, there was one apple less. So the King ordered a watch to be kept every night to discover who might be taking his golden apples.

Now the King had three sons. On the first night, his eldest son sat beneath the tree. But when it was almost midnight, that son could not keep from falling asleep. Next morning, another apple was gone.

Then the King's second son sat beneath the tree. But, as the clock was striking twelve, he too fell fast asleep. Next morning, yet another apple was gone.

Now it was the youngest son's turn to watch, but the King had little faith that he would succeed where his older brothers had failed. Yet that young man did not let sleep get the better of him. When twelve struck, he was still awake and watching. Soon something rustled overhead.

In the moonlight, the youngest son saw a large bird flying toward the tree. Its feathers were all made of gold. The bird landed on a branch and plucked off an apple just as the youngest son shot an arrow at it. The bird flew off, but the arrow had struck its plumage. One golden feather fell to earth.

The youngest son took it to the King and told what he had seen.

"That rascal is none other than the beautiful Golden Bird that was stolen from my garden long ago," the King said. "He must be found and brought back to me."

So the eldest and cleverest son set out. He thought he would easily find the Golden Bird. When he had traveled a short way, he saw a fox sitting at the edge of the woods. So he lifted his gun and took aim.

"Do not shoot me," cried the Fox, "and I will give you good advice about finding the Golden Bird. This evening you will come to a village with two inns. One will be brightly lit and filled with merrymaking, but do not go inside. Instead, stay at the other inn, though it will seem plain and dull."

"What a silly animal to give a wise fellow like me advice," thought the eldest son, and he pulled the trigger. He missed the Fox, who ran quickly into the woods.

Sure enough, by evening the first son had come to the village with the two inns. In one, every light was lit, and there was singing and dancing. The other had a poor, neglected look.

"Only a fool would go into that shabby inn," thought the eldest son. So he marched straightaway into the cheerful inn, joined in the pleasure and merrymaking and forgot all about looking for the Golden Bird.

When months passed and no news came, the second son set out to find the Golden Bird. Again the Fox appeared and offered the same good advice. Again the second brother paid no heed. When he saw his elder brother dancing by the window of the well-lit inn, he joined him there. He too lived only for pleasure and forgot all about the Golden Bird.

When several more months passed with no news, the King's youngest son begged to be allowed to seek the Golden Bird. At first the King refused. "How will a young know-nothing succeed where his older, wiser brothers have failed?" he asked. But at last he let the boy go.

Again the Fox appeared and offered the same advice. Being good-natured and modest, the youngest son was happy to listen.

"You won't be sorry," replied the Fox. "And, to get there more quickly, come sit on my bushy tail." Hardly was the young man seated when the fox began to run like the wind. When they came to the village, the lad saw the two inns and followed the Fox's counsel. He spend a peaceful night at the dark, quiet inn.

Next morning, the youngest son continued on his way. As soon as he left the town, the Fox appeared and said, "I will tell you what to do next. Ahead lies the castle of the king who stole your father's bird. Outside, it is guarded by a regiment of soldiers, but don't worry. They will all be sound asleep and snoring.

"Go straight into the castle, passing through every room until you come to the one where the Golden Bird rests inside a plain wooden cage. But take care. There stands a splendid, empty golden cage nearby. You must not move the Golden Bird from its plain cage into the fine one, or things will go badly."

Again the fox shook out his bushy tail, and the King's son sat upon it. Lickety split, they flew through the woods to the castle.

It all happened exactly as the Fox had said. But when the youngest son saw the two cages, he thought, "How sad to leave the Golden Bird in so common and ugly a cage." So he opened the door and moved the Golden Bird into the beautiful Golden Cage.

No sooner had he done this than the bird cried out, the soldiers woke and the young man was dragged off to the dungeon. Next morning he was sentenced to death.

But the king of the castle offered to spare the lad's life on one condition: he must bring him the Golden Horse that ran faster than the wind. If he succeeded, he would be given the Golden Bird as his reward.

With a heavy heart the youngest son set out. Once again, he met his friend, the Fox.

"See what comes of not taking good advice," said the Fox. "But all is not yet lost. Listen well, and I will tell you how to find the Golden Horse."

The King's youngest son was grateful and promised this time to heed the Fox's words.

"Straight ahead," explained the Fox, "lies a castle whose stable holds the Golden Horse. A dozen grooms lie in front of the stable, but they will be asleep and snoring. Go straight to the stall and lead the Golden Horse right by them. But be sure to put the worn leather saddle on the Golden Horse, not the shining gold one that hangs close by. Otherwise, things will go badly."

It all happened exactly as the Fox said. Yet, when the young man saw the beautiful, golden saddle, he could not help thinking, "What a shame to waste so splendid a saddle." So he threw the saddle of gold — and not the one of worn leather — across the horse's back. No sooner had he done so than the horse neighed loudly. The grooms awoke, seized the lad and tossed him into a dungeon. Next morning he was sentenced to death.

But the king of the castle promised to spare his life — and give him the Golden Horse into the bargain — if he would rescue the Beautiful Princess imprisoned in the Golden Castle.

"The Beautiful Princess is my promised bride," said this king. "Her wicked guardian keeps her locked away from me."

Once more the youngest son set out, and once more he met the trusty Fox. "Twice you have not listened," said the Fox, "and yet I will help you again. This road we are on leads straight to the Golden Castle. When evening comes and all is quiet, the Beautiful Princess will come to bathe in the bathhouse in the castle yard. Before she enters it, you must run up and kiss her. Then she will follow you, and you can carry her off. But remember this: you must not let her say goodbye to anyone in the castle."

The youngest son promised to heed the Fox's words, and, lickety-split, they were off yet again.

When they reached the Golden Castle, it was exactly as the Fox had said. When, at last, the Beautiful Princess came into the courtyard and walked toward the bathhouse, the lad sprang out and kissed her. At once she agreed to go where he took her, asking only to say goodbye to her guardian.

The youngest son said no, but when the Beautiful Princess wept, at last he said yes. No sooner had the Beautiful Princess reached her guardian's room than the young man was taken prisoner yet again and sentenced to death.

The guardian said he would spare the youngest son's life on one condition: he must take away the high hill that blocked the view from the guardian's window. "And you must do this in eight days," he said. "If you succeed, the Beautiful Princess is yours. If not, you forfeit your life."

The youngest son had no hope but began nonetheless to dig with a shovel. This time, no fox appeared. On the seventh day, when the lad saw how little he had done, he began to sob.

That night, the Fox appeared yet again. "You don't deserve my help," said the Fox. "Yet you have worked so hard that I will finish the job. Go to sleep."

Next morning when the youngest son awoke, the hill was gone! When the guardian saw that the task was done, he kept his word.

How happy the young man was to set forth with the Beautiful Princess. But when he told her that she was to be the bride of the king who owned the Golden Horse, she wept and wailed. She had not been promised to him and refused to be his bride. She wanted only to go home with the youngest son. "Besides," she said, "the Golden Horse doesn't even belong to that wicked king. It was stolen from me. It's mine."

The youngest son did not know what to do. Again, the good Fox appeared. "If the Princess chooses you, then she must be yours," said the Fox. "Now go and recover her Golden Horse."

"But how can I get the horse, yet keep the Princess?" said the young man. "That scoundrel of a king has a castle full of soldiers."

"First," said the Fox, "take the Princess to the king. Then he will lead forth the Golden Horse in exchange. Get on it immediately, then take the princess by the hand, swing her up onto the horse and gallop away. No one will be able to catch you."

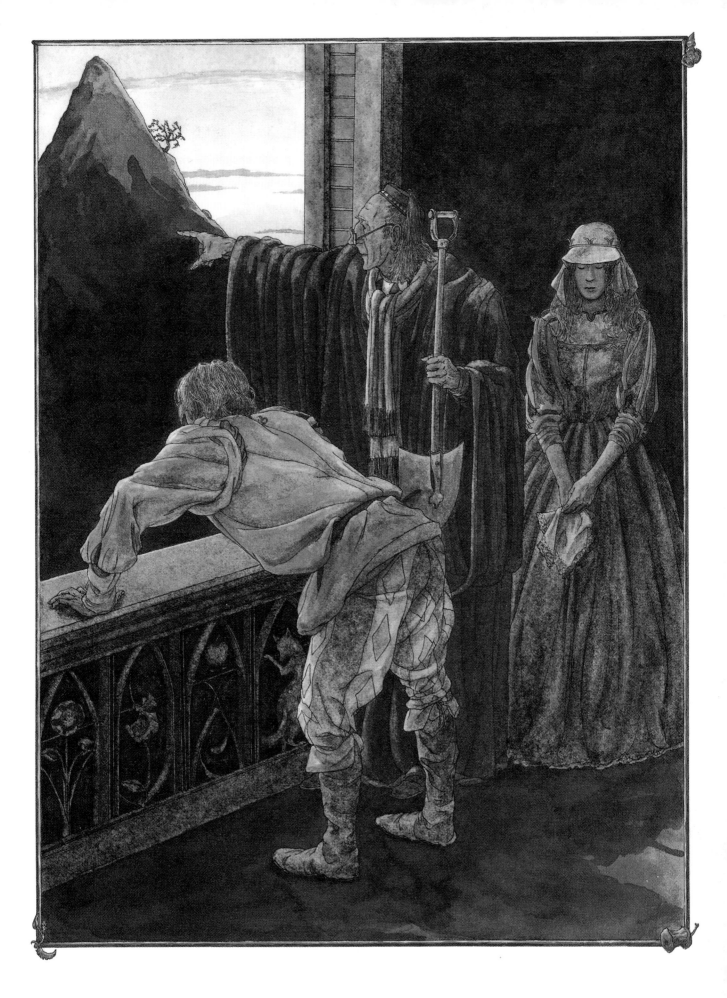

It happened exactly as the Fox said. "Now I will help you to recover your father's Golden Bird," the Fox promised. "When we come near to the castle, let the Princess stay with me. Then ride the Golden Horse boldly into the castle yard. When the Golden Bird is brought forth in exchange, seize the cage in your hand and gallop away like the wind."

It happened exactly as the Fox said. Now the King's youngest son was ready to ride home with all his wondrous treasures.

"I have one last piece of advice," said the Fox. "Beware of two things: don't stop to help any thief or other wrongdoer, and don't, whatever you do, sit at the edge of any well." With that the Fox ran off.

The youngest son's path took him through the village where his brothers had remained. There was a great noise when he arrived. Two men were about to be hanged. When the youngest son came to the place of the hanging, he saw that the two men were his brothers! At once he asked if there were any way in which he might save them, whatever their wrongdoing. "If you buy their freedom," answered the innkeeper. "But why waste your money on these penniless loafers? They aren't worth it."

The youngest son did not hesitate. He paid handsomely for his brothers' freedom and they were released. Soon they all came to the edge of the wood where the Fox had first met them. And, at that place, there was a well. Without stopping to think, the young man sat on its edge to rest.

In a moment, the two older brothers had pushed him backwards into the well. Then they seized the Beautiful Princess, the Golden Horse and the Golden Bird and rode straight home to their father. They told the Princess they would kill her if she dared to tell the truth.

"Father," they said, "we bring you not only the Golden Bird but the Golden Horse and the Beautiful Princess from the Golden Castle." The King believed them and rejoiced greatly.

Meanwhile, the youngest son had fallen into a deep, dry well. He wasn't hurt, but he could not climb out.

Once more, the faithful Fox appeared and leapt down beside the lad. "Yet again, you have not listened," the Fox said. "You have but one last chance to follow my advice. Still, if you obey, you may yet be happy.

"Your brothers have set watchers in the wood," said the Fox. "They are to kill you if you get out of the well. So you must change clothes with the man who is cutting wood at the roadside. Then no one will recognize you, and you can pass safely into the castle. But remember to wear your poor clothes until you are safe in your father's presence."

One last time, the Fox bade the youngest son to grasp his tail and hold on tight. Then he pulled him up out of the well.

It happened exactly as the Fox said. The lad changed clothes with the woodcutter and, in this way, arrived safely at his father's castle.

How he longed to change his poor clothes for fine ones, but he remembered the Fox's advice. No man knew who he was, and his older brothers never dreamed that he was in the castle.

Suddenly the Golden Bird began to sing, the Golden Horse began to eat and the Beautiful Princess stopped weeping.

"How happy I am," she said. "I feel as if my true bridegroom is nearby." And she felt so full of courage that she told the King the true story of the older brothers' treachery.

At once the King commanded everyone in the castle to come before him. Among them was the lad in ragged clothes. The Princess recognized him at once and threw her arms about him.

The wicked brothers were banished from the Kingdom, and the youngest son married the Beautiful Princess. The Fox remained their friend, and they all lived happily ever after.